D1046780

GHOST DETECTORS

I Dare You!

BOOK 4

BY
DOTTI ENDERLE

ILLUSTRATED BY
HOWARD MCWILLIAM

magic
wagon

FX
4115

visit us at www.abdopublishing.com

A special thanks to Melissa Markham — DE
For my sister Zoe — HM

Published by Magic Wagon, a division of the ABDO Group, 8000 West 78th Street, Edina, Minnesota 55439. Copyright © 2010 by Abdo Consulting Group, Inc. International copyrights reserved in all countries. All rights reserved. No part of this book may be reproduced in any form without written permission from the publisher.

Calico Chapter Books™ is a trademark and logo of Magic Wagon.

Printed in the United States of America, North Mankato, Minnesota.
012010
102013

Text by Dotti Enderle
Illustrations by Howard McWilliam
Edited by Stephanie Hedlund and Rochelle Baltzer
Cover and interior design by Jaime Martens

Library of Congress Cataloging-in-Publication Data

Enderle, Dotti, 1954-
   I dare you! / by Dotti Enderle ; illustrated by Howard McWilliam.
      p. cm. -- (Ghost Detectors ; bk. 4)
   Summary: At the county fair, ten-year-olds Malcolm and Dandy face a real ghost in the Screaming Mansion, while at home, Malcolm's sister Cocoa's attempt to become Fair Queen has the family in turmoil.
   ISBN 978-1-60270-693-4
   [1. Ghosts--Fiction. 2. Haunted places--Fiction. 3. Fairs--Fiction. 4. Family life--Fiction. 5. Humorous stories.] I. McWilliam, Howard, 1977- ill. II. Title.
   PZ7.E69645Iad 2009
   [Fic]--dc22
                                        2008055330

Contents

Three-Day Weekend

Malcolm peeked up at the school clock. It was two fifty.

"Just ten more minutes," his best friend, Dandy, whispered.

Their teacher, Mrs. Goolsby, smiled at the class. "You can start gathering your things," she announced.

That caused the classroom to spin into a race. Pencils, pens, and lunch boxes were eagerly being crammed into backpacks.

"And because we have a three-day weekend," Mrs. Goolsby continued, "I won't be assigning any homework."

The class burst into a loud, rowdy cheer. "Thank you!" Malcolm said out loud.

When Mrs. Goolsby didn't assign homework, it was a major event.

"I thought it would be pointless," she said. "You're all going to be at the fair anyway."

This caused another explosive cheer from the class. Everyone was excited for the annual Franklin County Fair.

Malcolm watched the clock slowly tick-tock its way to dismissal. Tomorrow was County Fair Day, celebrating the opening of the annual Franklin County Fair. After what felt like the longest seconds of his life, the bell finally rang.

Malcolm and Dandy wasted no time climbing into the school bus. They were ready to begin the bumpy journey that would start a three-day weekend of awesomeness.

"Okay," Malcolm said. "I've planned it all out."

Dandy, still chewing on his juice straw from lunch, listened. He continued working the straw around in his mouth even though it was mostly mush now.

"We'll get there as soon as it opens tomorrow," Malcolm went on. "Once we buy our tickets, we'll go to the left."

"But all the good stuff is to the right!" Dandy protested.

"I know," Malcolm said, "but everyone will go right. They'll start forming long lines right away. If we go left, then we

can get to the back rides before everyone else."

Dandy wiggled the flattened straw up and down. "That makes sense, I guess. I'm going to ride the Turbo Drop at least five times tomorrow," Dandy said.

"The Turbo Drop makes you throw up!"

"Only the first time," Dandy said.

The bus hit a bump, causing the straw to flip out of Dandy's mouth and onto his lap. He picked it back up and bit down.

Malcolm's mind was whirring, thinking of all the carnival rides. "We're definitely going on the Star Ship, Pirate's Fury, and the Scorpion."

"And the House of Mirrors," Dandy reminded him. "I like the one that squashes you up like a bug."

"Yeah, that's pretty cool." Malcolm remembered another house at the carnival. It had always been one of his favorites. "And we'll have to go into the Screaming Mansion. Even though it's probably not all that scary anymore."

Malcolm had already had several encounters with real ghosts, including his great-grandfather Bertram and his pet dog, Spooky. So how scary could a carnival haunted house be?

"It's the jump-out moments that scare the bejeebbers out of me," Dandy said.

The bus turned onto Dandy's street. Dandy removed the straw from his mouth and tucked it into his pocket. "I'm just happy that I get to sleep in."

Ugh! Malcolm wished he could sleep in. "I have to go to the fair parade in the morning," he said.

Dandy made a face. "That's just a bunch of boring stuff like the mayor and the high school band. Oh, and that one-horned goat they call a unicorn. And those goofy girls running for Fair Queen."

"Yeah," Malcolm said, "that's why I have to go. My sister is one of those goofy girls!"

Cocoa for Fair Queen

Malcolm tried to digest his dinner that night, but his sister, Cocoa, made it impossible.

"It's a disaster!" she moaned, gripping the door frame like she needed medical attention. "I can't find my sapphire earrings, my raspberry lip gloss has dried up, and there's a huge crease in my taffeta dress!" She drooped against the wall like she was about to faint.

Malcolm glanced at his dad, who stared down at his food. They'd both learned a long time ago not to get involved in girl matters. Grandma Eunice kept her head down, too. She stabbed at her macaroni and cheese like it might escape her plate.

Malcolm's mom pointed to the "Cocoa for Fair Queen" flyer stuck on the refrigerator with a magnet. "Why don't you wear the dress you wore in the photo?" she suggested.

Cocoa's eyes grew twice their size. She jerked up tall, clutching the door frame with a kung-fu grip. Malcolm braced himself for the explosion.

"What!?!" she screamed. "I can't wear the same dress! Everyone will laugh at me!" Her volume was on high, but she had difficulty forming words. Then Malcolm saw the whitening strips she had on both her upper and lower teeth.

"Then we'll steam the wrinkle out of the dress," Mom proposed.

"It's more than a wrinkle," Cocoa said. "It's a canyon."

Grandma Eunice placed a hunk of macaroni noodles in her mouth. "Remember when we all went to the Grand Canyon?"

"Grandma!" Cocoa sobbed. "We're dealing with a crisis right now."

Grandma nodded. "I rode a donkey."

Malcolm had never been to the Grand Canyon. But, he remembered seeing a picture of Grandma Eunice on a donkey, scaling the canyon slopes.

"That's it, Cocoa," Malcolm said. "You're sure to win if you ride in on a donkey."

"You are a donkey!" she yelled back.

Dad looked him in the eyes, silently shaking his head. Malcolm knew it was the reminder to stay out of it.

Mom tried to get things under control. "Why don't you sit down and eat? Then we'll take care of things."

Cocoa gritted her teeth, pointing to the strips she'd plastered on. "I have to keep these on for thirty minutes," she said.

Malcolm knew it would make more sense if she used the strips after dinner. But when did Cocoa ever make sense?

"I tried those whitening strips once," Grandma Eunice offered. "They didn't work at all."

"Because they don't work on false teeth," Cocoa said, rolling her eyes.

Mom sighed. "Honey, stop worrying. Especially about the dress."

"But what about my lip gloss?" she argued.

"We'll run to the store after dinner and buy a new tube."

"And my earrings?" Cocoa asked.

Grandma Eunice pointed her fork in Cocoa's direction. "You can use my earrings." A noodle flipped off the fork and sailed across the table.

"Oh, Grandma! You're earrings are the size of boulders!"

Grandma turned back to her plate. "They have some interesting boulders at the Grand Canyon."

"I know," Malcolm said.

Grandma winked. "And they're best viewed when riding a donkey."

"Aaaarrrrrgh!" Cocoa screamed. She

pivoted and stomped down the hall. "I'm going to straighten my hair!"

Cocoa's hair always had that Bride of Frankenstein quality. So Malcolm knew that she'd be gone awhile.

"Remember," Mom said, "the parade starts at nine in the morning. We have to be there at seven thirty."

"Seven thirty?" Malcolm made a small grunting noise to show his disapproval. "Do I have to go?" he asked.

"Yes," Mom and Dad said together.

"Besides," Mom said with a glint, "Cocoa will be riding in a lovely white convertible. She's going to be breathtaking."

"Yeah. I'll be laughing so hard I won't be able to breathe."

"Be nice," Mom warned.

"I rode in a convertible once," Grandma Eunice said.

"Really?" Mom asked. "When was that?"

"When I was at the Grand Canyon," she answered. "That donkey didn't have a roof."

Malcolm laughed, sputtering mac and cheese back onto his plate. He managed to get a few more bites in before the entire house shook.

"Mom!" Cocoa screamed from the bathroom. "My straightener isn't working!"

Malcolm knew it was going to be a long night.

I Dare You

The parade was pretty much as Malcolm expected. Balloons and confetti floated in the air. Marching bands tried to march around the clumps that the horses had left.

Cocoa managed to get her hair, makeup, dress, and fingernails to match perfectly. "I'll really stand out in that white convertible!" she announced.

But the convertible had a flat tire right before the parade started. Cocoa was

forced to smile and wave from inside a black and green clown jalopy. Mom spent an hour trying to console her afterward.

The Franklin County Fair opened its gates at three o'clock. Malcolm and Dandy had been in line since two thirty.

"How many?" the ticket clerk asked.

The boys slapped their money down. "Wristbands, please," Malcolm said.

The clerk attached a sky blue band to each boy's left wrist.

"Let's go!" Dandy shouted, rushing inside.

"To the left," Malcolm reminded him.

They rushed past the food area—booths of cotton candy, funnel cakes, and sausages on sticks. They hurried by the barbecue pits, burger stands, and boiling pots of five-alarm chili.

They whizzed around the stage that held a banner reading:

TONIGHT at 8:00 pm
★ ★ ★ ★ ★ ★ ★ ★ ★ ★
Cactus Jim and His Prickly Pickers

After they'd gotten by the little kiddy rides, they were the first in line for the Anti-gravity Chamber.

"Awesome!" Malcolm cheered.

Once their feet were planted firmly on the ground, they rode the Star Ship, the Scorpion, and the Runaway Coaster. The lines got longer as they made their way around. But the longest line formed in front of the Screaming Mansion.

"Think we should go in?" Dandy asked.

Malcolm shrugged. "Why not?"

They took their place in the back of the line.

The Screaming Mansion was nothing more than a wooden cutout placed in front of an oversized trailer. How scary could it be?

The Mansion's overseer was a short man with shaggy brown hair and scruffy whiskers. The sleeves of his denim shirt were rolled up to the elbows, and he wore a peeling name tag that said *Gus*. Gus would open the rope and let a few people in at a time.

Malcolm kept his eyes on the exit. He wanted to see the faces of those who'd braved their way through.

Instead of excitement and chatter, the folks coming out of the Screaming Mansion held their hands over their hearts. Some were in tears, including the guys.

Dandy looked at Malcolm and swallowed hard. "It must be scarier this year."

As they neared the rope, Gus cocked his eyebrow and whispered, "Think you can handle it?"

Malcolm laughed. "Piece of cake."

Dandy gulped again. "How scary is it?" Dandy had turned a sickly shade of green. Of course that could have been from riding the Anti-gravity Chamber earlier.

Gus spit on the ground and said, "I won't even go in there."

"I've seen real ghosts," Malcolm informed him.

"So have I," Gus said, cocking the other eyebrow.

Just then, a boy came screaming out of the exit and rushed straight to the men's room.

"Your last chance," Gus said, his hand on the rope latch.

Dandy stepped to the side. "I ch-changed my mind."

Malcolm grabbed Dandy's arm. "Wait. He's just trying to scare us. It's part of the attraction."

Gus unlatched the rope. "Go on in." Then he leaned closer. "I dare you."

Enter at Your Own Risk

Malcolm gripped Dandy by the collar and led him through the Mansion's crooked door. They entered the usual dark hallway. A lone black light shone down on a plastic skeleton that pointed the way.

"It's just the same as last year," Dandy said.

Malcolm agreed. But last year people exited with smiles on their faces. What could be so scary this time?

They rounded a corner and ducked. A large, furry bat flew down from the rafters, brushing against their heads. It could've been a "jump out of your pants" moment, except the electric motor inside the bat was whirring much too loudly. And the cable holding it glowed neon from the lighting. Malcolm swatted at it.

Dandy stood a little taller. "This is nothing," he said, boldly. "Why do you think that guy dared us to go in?"

"He was just trying to build up tension," Malcolm answered. "Make it scarier."

It was then that a witch with a nose the size and color of a green banana poked her head through a fake window. "Would you like to stay for a spell?" her mechanical voice asked. One of the bulbs in her red glowing eyes had dimmed to a shell pink.

The boys inched their way along. "Remember," Malcolm said, "when we get to the next door, a werewolf dummy will step out."

On cue, the werewolf, in his ragged shirt and pants, flung back the door and jumped out at them. "Grrrrrr!"

Dandy growled back.

Rounding the next corner, they saw a coffin up ahead. Dandy stopped. "I forget, is that Dracula or the mummy?"

Malcolm had been through this spook house so many times he had it memorized. "Dracula. The mummy's coffin is standing up."

Just as they were passing it, the coffin lid flew open and Dracula sat straight up. His voiced echoed a "Velcome!" His red eyes glowed brighter than the witch's.

Dandy crossed his index fingers in front of him as they passed. "No vampire's gonna get us," Dandy said.

Malcolm laughed. "Not in here anyway."

By now Malcolm was yawning. Could this place be more boring? He remembered when he couldn't get through this thing without holding someone's hand. Or maybe it was just the fact that Malcolm had seen much scarier things since the last time he'd come here.

A couple of spotlights circled around them. Malcolm laughed. "Remember when we thought those were real ghosts?"

Dandy laughed too.

The mummy fell forward from its tomb, real flakes of decay falling from his rags.

"I think that's the last thing," Malcolm said. But just as he said it, a large black cat slinked forward and arched its back. *Hssssssss!*

"Wow, that's new," Dandy observed. When he reached down to touch it, the cat took a swipe at his hand. Little beads of blood formed on the scratches.

"Ouch! It's real!"

The cat continued to hiss. Dandy held his hurt hand and backed against the wall. "Is it part of the spook house?"

Malcolm wasn't sure. "Here, kitty, kitty." He leaned forward, but the cat kept hissing. "Maybe it just wandered in."

"Can we get around it?" Dandy asked.

"Maybe," Malcolm said and shrugged.

They were just a few feet from the exit door. The cat charged, swiping the air.

Malcolm and Dandy both inched along, their backs plastered to the wall. "Nice kitty. Nice kitty," they chanted.

Just as they reached the exit, the door slammed shut. Malcolm grabbed the handle and tugged. "It's locked!"

Both boys grabbed it, yanking hard.

Something crept up from behind. They turned slowly.

A woman stood over them. Her hair floated like a mermaid's. One eye drooped lower than the other. And she had a mouth full of black, rotting teeth.

"You touched my cat!" she screamed. Her breath reminded Malcolm of the time his mom left the fish sticks in the microwave too long.

"It touched us!" Dandy argued. "Let us out!"

The hag drew even closer. "You shouldn't be in my house!"

Dandy held up his arm and showed her his wristband. "We paid to get in."

"And you'll pay again!" she fumed.

Sparks flew from her fingertips, shocking Malcolm and Dandy's arms and legs.

"Ouch! Ouch!" It stung like getting zapped with a trick hand buzzer.

"This isn't funny," Malcolm said, trying to defend himself. "Open the door!"

He reached out to knock the woman's hand away, but his arm went right through her.

"Dandy," Malcolm said, his heart in this throat. "This isn't part of the spook house. This is a real ghost!"

Closed!

The ghost flew up, hovering above them. Her drooping eye sagged lower on her face.

Dandy struggled with the door handle. "Let us out! Let us out!"

Malcolm stood, waiting. Was the ghost going to drop down on them?

She floated closer . . . closer . . . her face twisting. "I'm ready for my close-up, Mr. DeMille."

Malcolm had no idea who Mr. DeMille was, but he wanted no part of this ghost's close-up. And just as her face came within inches of his, the door flew open, sending him and Dandy falling in a heap.

A man in a green striped shirt and a gold bow tie pushed his way in. "Everyone out!" he ordered. Malcolm looked behind him. He and Dandy were the only ones inside.

They didn't waste time stumbling out the door. It was great to be outside! But Malcolm could hear the ghost inside, sadly singing "If They Could See Me Now."

The man with the bow tie locked the spook house door. "Closed until further notice," he announced.

"That's fine with me!" Dandy said, rubbing his scraped hand.

"Why are you closing it?" Malcolm asked. It seemed obvious, but Malcolm wanted to hear the man's explanation.

"Too many complaints," Mr. Bow Tie answered. "The Screaming Mansion is causing more than screams. Two people fainted and one claims that something inside there twisted his nose. A few more fussed about noogies and wet willies. It's just not safe in there."

Dandy held out his hand. "Yeah, look what happened to me."

Malcolm noticed that the scratches weren't really that deep. Still, the man's face looked panicked. "Oh dear," Mr. Bow Tie sighed.

"There's a real live cat inside," Malcolm told him. "I think it might be hungry."

"We'll check on that." The man's face suddenly switched on a smile. "Tell you

what, young man," he said to Dandy. "You go to the ticket window tomorrow and tell Myrna that Frank sent you. You can ride for free all day."

"Wow, thanks!" Dandy said.

Frank and his bow tie shuffled off.

Malcolm and Dandy headed for the restroom. In the distance they could hear banjo music as Cactus Jim and His Prickly Pickers strummed a country jig. Was it after eight o'clock already?

Inside the men's room, Dandy scrubbed his hand with soap. "I gotta be careful," he said. "I had Cat Scratch Fever once. The glands in my armpits swelled up like popcorn."

Malcolm remembered that. Dandy had walked around like he still had the hanger stuck in his shirt.

"It was awful. I had to get a shot and take pills! I don't want to do that again."

Malcolm heard Dandy, but he wasn't really listening. He was trying to figure out what had just happened in the Screaming Mansion. "Dandy, we just saw a real ghost."

"Again!" Dandy reminded him. "It's like they're following us around."

"But we saw it without the specter detector."

During the summer, Malcolm had bought a wonderful gadget called the Ecto-Handheld-Automatic-Heat-Sensitive-Laser-Enhanced Specter Detector. And since getting it, he'd detected several ghosts. But Malcolm had left the specter detector at home.

"I think everybody saw it, Malcolm. Not just us. That's why they closed the

mansion." Dandy continued scrubbing his hand. A soap bubble floated upward, settling on the tip of his nose. His eyes crossed trying to look at it. When he reached up to pop it, a huge glop of soap stuck to his face.

Malcolm's brain was running in fast-forward. "Why is there a real ghost in a carnival spook house? Where'd she come from? What does she want?"

"Yeah . . . and who's Mr. DeMille?" Dandy wondered.

"I don't know, but that ghost is ruining the Screaming Mansion. When we come back tomorrow, we're bringing the ghost zapper."

A Clever Plan

"Where were you tonight?" Mom asked as Malcolm and Dandy came in the front door.

Malcolm heard some fierce shrieking.

"Near, far, wherever you are!" Cocoa sang in the next room. It sounded like a sick cow had wandered into the house.

Malcolm held his ears. "We were at the fair."

"I know you were at the fair," Mom replied. "Why weren't you at the introductions? The candidates read their essays on how they'd help the community as Fair Queen. Cocoa's was the best, of course."

Malcolm thought of lots of ways Cocoa could help the community. Wear a bag over her head. Move away. "Sorry," he mumbled. "I forgot."

"I forgot too," Grandma Eunice said, wheeling herself in. She had a can of soda in one hand and the TV remote in the other. Malcolm wondered how she managed to steer the wheelchair.

Mom sighed. "Grandma, you were there."

"Yes, I know. But I've already forgotten her essay. Something about riding a unicycle."

"No," Mom said. "She wants to help unite the community and encourage recycling."

"Well, she can start with this." Grandma Eunice took the last sip of her soda, then pitched it into a vase by the door. She gave Malcolm a secret wink.

The shrieking in the next room got higher and louder. "My heart will go on and on . . . " Cocoa was practicing for the talent portion of the Fair Queen pageant. And to make it worse, she was singing into a karaoke machine, magnifying the sound.

Mom pointed a finger at Malcolm. "Make sure you're there tomorrow night. That's when Cocoa sings."

Singing? Mom thought that yowling was actually music? "I'll remember."

Dandy, who'd just stood there twitching the whole time, followed Malcolm down to the basement lab. Shutting the door was a major relief to Malcolm's ears. "No way she's going to win singing like that," he said.

"I know," Dandy agreed. "She sounds like a hippo sitting on a hot stove."

Malcolm couldn't have put it better himself. He walked over to the beanbag chair, but instead of sitting, he moved it aside. Then Malcolm lifted a loose board from the floor. He retrieved a large box he had stashed underneath. Replacing the board, Malcolm sat down, pretzel style. The first thing he took from the box was his specter detector.

Dandy watched while picking at the scabs forming on his hand. "We won't be needing that."

"We will if we want to play with Spooky." Malcolm switched it on and waited.

Yip! Yip! Spooky, his ghost dog magically appeared. Spooky had followed Malcolm home earlier that summer.

Malcolm took out a flashlight and shined the beam on the wall. Spooky bounced, chasing the light as Malcolm swerved it around. Malcolm had tried using old socks and rubber balls to play with Spooky. But light was the only thing that he could actually catch.

"So what's the plan?" Dandy asked, squatting down to sit near Malcolm.

"I'm thinking," Malcolm said, circling the light across the basement floor. Spooky chased it round and round.

Dandy looked at his hand, then at Malcolm. "You know, we don't really

have to do anything. The fair will only be here for a couple of weekends. Then the carnival moves on. And the Screaming Mansion is a dumb attraction anyway."

Malcolm handed the flashlight to Dandy. "No. We have to take care of this. After all, that's what we do." He reached in the box and took out the ghost zapper. Spooky took one look, jumped through Dandy, then hid behind the beanbag.

The ghost zapper looked a lot like a can of whipped cream with a trigger. But Malcolm knew its power. During the summer he'd used it to turn an evil ghost into a puddle of liquid goo.

"But how will we get in?" Dandy asked. "Frank locked it up, remember?"

Malcolm grinned. "Don't worry. I thought of a plan."

Finding a Way In

Malcolm barely slept. His mind kept rolling over and over with questions. Who was the ghost? Why was she haunting a carnival haunted house? But he mostly wondered, why are ghosts always such a pain?

The fair opened at eleven o'clock. Malcolm and Dandy were there waiting.

"Frank sent us," Dandy told the ticket lady. He held out his hand. The scratches were now just a couple of pinkish lines.

Malcolm wasn't sure he deserved free admission. What happened in the Screaming Mansion had been scary and upsetting, but he hadn't suffered any bumps or bruises. But the woman yawned, nodded, and handed Dandy two wristbands.

Before heading through the gate, a guard stopped them. "I have to look inside your backpack."

Malcolm had forgotten about the safety check. He gave Dandy a nervous look, then shrugged off his backpack and opened it.

"What's this?" the guard asked, holding up the specter detector.

Malcolm had to think quick. "It's a prize I won yesterday."

The guard put it back, then pulled out the zapper. "And this?"

"There's my Silly String!" Dandy said, snatching it back. "I've been looking everywhere for this."

The guard handed Malcolm his backpack. "Just don't use that on anyone inside, okay?"

Dandy nodded.

"Wow, good call!" Malcolm said, once they'd passed through the gate.

Dandy looked at the can. "You mean this isn't my Silly String? Oh rats! I thought I'd found it." He handed it over to Malcolm.

"I'm just glad he didn't make a big deal about the cat food I have in there," Malcolm said.

This time, the boys went to the right after passing through the gates. They weren't stopping for any rides. The

Screaming Mansion loomed up ahead. It looked dark and abandoned.

Malcolm motioned quietly to Dandy. "Follow me," he whispered. Checking over his shoulder to make sure no one

saw, he stepped over a jumble of cables and slipped around to the back of the haunted house.

"But the entrance and exit are in the front," Dandy said. "Why are we back here?"

"Because there has to be another way in." Malcolm scanned the oversized trailer up and down. Nothing. Not even a window. "There has to be an emergency exit somewhere."

He got down on his knees, then crawled underneath. It was a tight squeeze with all the cables and cords. "It's dark under here," he called to Dandy.

Malcolm ran his hands along the bottom. He squirmed farther in. Then he saw it. A sagging square cut out of the bottom. A trapdoor? Malcolm wasn't

sure. "Dandy, look in my backpack and hand me the flashlight."

Malcolm waited.

"Dandy," he called. "My flashlight."

No answer.

"Ugh!" He'd have to retrieve it himself. Dandy must've gotten distracted by a passing clown. Or maybe the snake lady had come around back to avoid the crowd. Malcolm had no choice but to get the flashlight himself.

He didn't have much room to turn around, so he backed out. "Dandy!" he said, pulling himself up. "Why didn't you—" Malcolm froze. Standing next to Dandy, flashing a huge, toothy grin, was Gus.

Let's Make a Deal

Gus towered over them with hands on his hips. He had a toothpick in his mouth, working it up and down.

"Got ya."

Dandy just stood silently, like a kid who'd been caught with his finger in the cake icing. Malcolm tried to think of a way out.

"That's pretty dangerous, kid," Gus said, the toothpick bouncing between his yellow teeth.

Malcolm nodded. "I-I know. It's just that . . . I was looking for something." At least he wasn't lying. He waited for Dandy to come to his rescue, but Dandy was frozen, sweat beads on his nose.

Gus switched the toothpick to the other side of his mouth. "What do ya think Frank would say about all this?"

Dandy glanced at his free wristband. "Don't tell Frank. I promise, we won't do it again!"

Gus cocked an eyebrow. "Won't do what again?"

Uh-oh. Malcolm had to come up with something to get them out of this mess. "It's just that we left something inside yesterday. I was trying to find a way in."

Gus lifted his shirttail. A cluster of keys were attached to his belt loop. "Why didn't you ask?"

"You'll let us in?" Malcolm asked, less worried now.

"Sure. If you tell me what you're looking for."

Malcolm looked at Dandy. Dandy looked at Malcolm. Neither were quick to come up with an answer. Finally Malcolm said, "We want to feed the cat."

"No feeding the cat," Gus said. "We're trying to get it out of there."

"Can't you trap it?" Dandy asked.

"Tried," Gus answered, jiggling the toothpick. "It's too wild. It sneaks out and rummages through the food vendors' trash. Then it sneaks back in. We can't catch it."

"Maybe we can," Malcolm offered. He was seeing a great chance of getting in.

But Gus still gave him a piercing stare. "Is it really the cat you want to catch?"

Malcolm gulped. Should he tell Gus the truth?

"I know you saw her," Gus said. "Why do you think I dared you to go in?" That evil grin of his was back.

"Who is she?" Malcolm asked.

"I don't know," Gus said. "But she needs to go. Every time they close the Screaming Mansion I get stuck working the carousel. I hate working the baby rides."

"We can help," Malcolm told him. "We have the tools to get rid of her. If you would just let us in."

Gus scratched his head. "Wouldn't do any good right now."

"Why not?" Malcolm asked.

"Because she doesn't come out much during the day. Your best bet is to come back tonight. She's always in there at night."

Malcolm glanced over at Dandy. He looked like he'd swallowed a bug. "I'm not sure we can come back tonight," Malcolm said.

Gus jiggled the toothpick. "Chicken?"

"No," Malcolm argued. "It's not that." Actually, it was that. He'd much rather tackle a ghost in the daylight.

"Then come back tonight," Gus said. With a wicked smile he added, "I dare you."

"But what are we supposed to do till then?" Dandy asked him.

Gus pointed to Dandy's wristband. "Have fun." Then he walked off.

All in Good Time

"So what now?" Dandy asked, scratching his chin. The boys headed back into the carnival crowd.

"We'll do what Gus said," Malcolm answered. "Let's have fun."

Malcolm looked down at his watch. It was an advanced digital wristwatch that looked like it'd been designed by NASA. The watch displayed the time in every time zone. It also showed the temperature and had a panic alarm and a laser pointer.

But it mostly showed him what he already knew. It was hours until sundown!

They took a turn on every ride, winding their way back around to the hot dog stand. They passed the stage, which was decorated with silver streamers and glittered stars. It displayed a new banner.

TONIGHT AT 8:00 PM

Franklin County Fair Queen

Talent Competition

The boys sat down with their hot dogs and colas.

"This is going to be tricky," Malcolm said, taking a bite of his chili cheese dog. "We have to zap that ghost and be back here by eight. Mom will kill me if I miss Cocoa's performance."

Dandy had about fifteen packets of ketchup. He ripped into each one with his teeth and squirted it on his hot dog. A lot of it missed and hit the tabletop. "That is going to be tricky. It doesn't get dark until about seven thirty."

Malcolm sipped his drink. "I think we can manage it. If Gus lets us in as soon as it's dark."

Dandy squeezed another ketchup packet. Some of it hit his hot dog. The rest spurted out in a thin red line across the table. "Do you think Gus will let us in?"

Malcolm nodded. "They've got him working the pony rides now. Didn't you see him? The guy looks like he just lost his best friend."

"He did look pretty gloomy."

"Wouldn't you?" Malcolm asked. "Not only does he have to lead those ponies in a circle, but he also has to do poop patrol."

"Ugh!" Dandy said, spattering ketchup all over his drink cup. "I hated doing that when we dog sat. I sure wouldn't want to shovel up poop from a bunch of ponies."

"Yeah, Gus was cut out for bigger things than that. They could have at least put him on bumper car duty."

"If I worked for the carnival, that's where I'd want to be," Dandy said. He finally picked up his hot dog, only to have the bun disintegrate into a pile of pink goo.

"Gus will definitely be there at sundown," Malcolm told him. He checked his watch one more time. Still a few hours left.

"So what do you want to do next?" Dandy asked, managing a bite that smeared ketchup and crumbs on his face.

Malcolm shrugged. "Let's do the bumper cars again."

Dandy grinned through his ketchup-blotched lips. "Cool."

Taking Action

Malcolm and Dandy had managed to ride everything twice, share a funnel cake, and win a squirt gun and a giant foam finger at the game counters. A cool wind breezed through as the sun sank behind the carnival stage. Malcolm looked at his watch.

"Let's go," he said. He and Dandy made their way to the Screaming Mansion.

It looked extra creepy in the dusky shadows. The fairground was well lit

with flashing strobes and neon lights. Yet the darkened spook house seemed all alone among the cheering crowds passing by. The boys ducked under a chain that blocked the path leading up to it. They hid in a corner near the entrance.

"Where's Gus?" Malcolm asked, looking back and forth.

Dandy looked around too. "Maybe he had poop patrol."

"We need to get in there quick. Cocoa goes on stage soon."

They waited. Malcolm glanced at his watch again. Dandy put on the giant foam finger.

"Where is he?" Malcolm whispered impatiently. It had only been a minute, but it felt like hours. He felt antsy. His right knee twitched. Then this left. He shifted his backpack from one shoulder to

the other. That's when Dandy pointed the spongy finger. "There he is!"

Gus made his way through the crowd and under the roping. "Sorry," he said. "I couldn't get anyone to cover for me. I had to put an out-of-order sign on the pony ride."

"How can ponies be out of order?" Dandy asked.

"Well, they have to eat sometime," Gus answered. Carefully scanning the area, he fished his keys out and unlocked the padlock on the door. "Good luck," he said, pushing open the squeaky door.

Malcolm gazed into the pitch-black hallway. "Aren't you going to turn on some lights?"

"Can't," Gus said. "They're all connected. Every light will come on. Folks will think it's open for business."

"Well, it will be soon," Malcolm said with confidence. He opened his pack and took out a flashlight and his ghost detector. He and Dandy headed inside.

Malcolm switched the ghost detector on. It powered up. Then he turned it to Detect.

"Where are you?" Malcolm whispered, taking one step at a time.

Dandy squeezed his hand into the glove part of the foam finger. "Here kitty, kitty, kitty."

Bleep . . . bleep . . . bleep . . . bleep . . .

The specter detector showed no activity.

Malcolm shone the flashlight on each of the mechanical characters as they passed.

"Wow," Dandy said, his voice shaky.

"Dracula and the Wolfman look scary even without their flashing red eyes."

They inched farther along. When they rounded the next corner, something jumped down from the mummy's tomb. *Hisssssssssssssssss!*

"Boy, that cat sure likes the mummy!" Dandy said, poking at it with the foam finger. The cat took a few swats at it. "Nana-nana-na-na!" Dandy teased. "You're not going to get me again." The cat leaped, latching onto Dandy's arm. "Ouch!"

Malcolm set the cat food down, then popped open the lid. The cat let go of Dandy and began scarfing down the food.

Purrrrrrrrrrrrr

"See?" Malcolm said. "It's really a nice kitty."

Dandy looked at the red spots on his arm. "When he's not clawing you to pieces."

Malcolm reached down and petted the cat. "We're going to get you to an animal shelter," he said.

Purrrrrrrrrrrrrrr

"Wow, it's really purring loud now," Dandy said.

Malcolm looked around. "Wait . . . that's not just the cat." Then he looked down at his ghost detector.

Bleeeeeeeeeeeeeeeeeeeeeeeeeeeeep!

True Talent

The droopy-eyed ghost hovered just above them. "I told you not to touch my cat!"

"Quick!" Malcolm yelled to Dandy. "Get the zapper!"

Dandy fumbled with the backpack, not making any progress.

"Take off that foam finger!" Malcolm shouted.

The ghost drifted closer, her hair

floating in all directions. "You don't belong here!" she fumed.

"Neither do you!" Malcolm countered. "Hurry," he whispered to Dandy.

The ghost stopped. Her entire face drooped. "You're right," she said. "You're right," she repeated, this time with a sob.

She backed away, drying her ghostly tears. "I should be haunting a movie studio. Or the backstage of a Broadway theater. I should've been a star!"

Dandy stopped digging through the backpack and looked up. "Really? 'Cause you don't look like a movie star."

"What do you know?" she screeched. "I had talent. I could sing, dance, act—a triple threat. And I could juggle."

"What happened?" Malcolm dared to ask. He gave Dandy a signal to get the zapper.

"What happened? I got a few bit parts in the chorus now and then, but never a starring role. I worked hard. But, I ran out of money after a few years. I needed a job, so I was forced to work as a carnie."

"You worked for the carnival?" Malcolm asked as Dandy slipped the zapper into his hand.

"Yes!" she shrilled, sounding threatening again. "And I could never get out. Never! I'm stuck here."

"Not for long," Malcolm said. He whipped the zapper around from behind him and hit the trigger. But the ghost was quicker. She flew through the wall of the Screaming Mansion.

Malcolm ran for the back door.

"We've got to get her!" He pushed it open, and they bolted out. "There she is!"

The ghost sailed through the field just outside the carnival activity. Malcolm and Dandy followed.

"She's fast," Dandy said, trying to keep up with Malcolm.

They circled behind the rides and games, trying not to lose sight of her. Malcolm kept the zapper in front of him, ready to fire.

The ghost led them all the way around to the stage area. That's when Malcolm heard the announcer say, "Welcome, Cocoa, singing 'My Heart Will Go On'."

Uh-oh! Malcolm thought. And right then, the ghost flew through the back of the stage and slammed into his sister.

"Where'd she go?" Dandy asked.

Malcolm looked around. "I don't know." But he noticed that Cocoa didn't

quite look herself. When the applause died down, a large smile appeared on her face. She began to sing an entirely different song.

"Won't you come home, Bill Bailey? Won't you come home? I know I done you wro-ung."

She did high kicks with jazz hands. She shuffled her feet. She spun in perfect circles, never missing a word of the song.

"Wow," Dandy said. "Your sister's really good."

Malcolm gave him a look. "That's not my sister."

The ghost inside of Cocoa finished. Then she held her arms up, relishing the thunderous applause.

"Thank you! Thank you!" she shouted, standing and bowing deeply. She even

blew kisses. The whole crowd was on its feet.

She continued to bow as she backed off the stage. Malcolm and Dandy hurried around to meet her. Cocoa eyed them, then fainted, leaving the ghost behind.

"That was your final curtain," Malcolm said, aiming the zapper.

"Wait!" the ghost begged. "They loved me. Did you hear it? They loved me!" The ghost looked longingly at Malcolm. "Please don't use whatever that thing is on me. I'll go away. I promise. I'll find an abandoned theater with other ghosts. We'll perform for each other. I'll be a headliner every night!"

Dandy looked at Malcolm. "She is pretty good."

"Yeah," Malcolm agreed. "It'd be a shame to zap such talent." He took his finger off the trigger. "Just make sure you leave the Screaming Mansion for good."

"You'll never see me again." And with that, the ghost evaporated.

Cocoa stirred. "Is it time to go on yet?"

Rescued

Malcolm rubbed the sleep from his eyes as he sat down for breakfast the next morning. Cocoa followed wearing yellow flannel pajamas with orange and pink striped socks. Her Fair Queen tiara was balanced high upon her head. She looked both dreamy and confused at the same time.

"I still don't remember it," she said, plopping down in a chair.

Malcolm's mom, who was flipping pancakes, sighed. "Honey, do we need to show you the video again?"

"But I don't even know that song!"

Grandma Eunice sipped her prune juice. "It's a dandy of a song," she said.

Mom retrieved some butter from the refrigerator. "Grandma, please don't sing at the table."

Grandma pushed her wheelchair about a foot away, still singing, "I know I done you wro-ung! Remember that rainy evening . . ."

Dad grunted from behind his newspaper.

"I just wish I could remember," Cocoa said. "It's like I wasn't even there."

Malcolm grinned. "Maybe that's why it was so good."

Cocoa stuck her tongue out at him.

That afternoon, Malcolm and Dandy went down to the basement lab. Malcolm turned on the specter detector so Spooky could play. *Yip! Yip!*

"Check this out," Malcolm said, handing Dandy the morning paper.

"You mean the article about your sister?"

Malcolm shook his head. "No. Below that."

Dandy's eyes glinted as he read.

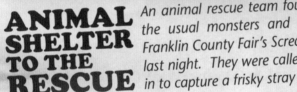

ANIMAL SHELTER TO THE RESCUE

An animal rescue team found more than the usual monsters and goblins in the Franklin County Fair's Screaming Mansion last night. They were called in to capture a frisky stray cat, but they uncovered much more! Tucked securely behind the mummy's tomb was a litter of mewing kittens. The mama cat and her babies are now safe at the Franklin County Animal Shelter.

Dandy looked down at the Band-Aid on his arm. "No wonder that cat was so mean."

"Yeah," Malcolm said. "It was just trying to protect its kittens."

"So what about the ghost?" Dandy asked. "Think she'll keep her promise?"

Malcolm shrugged. "Probably. She'll be performing on the other side from now on."

"I'm kind of bored. Want to go do something?" Dandy asked Malcolm.

Malcolm thought about it. "We can always go back to the fair."

"Yeah," Dandy said. "We still have time to ride everything twice more."

Malcolm switched off the specter detector and grinned. "Let's start with the Screaming Mansion."

FIVE MORE WAYS TO DETECT A GHOST, SPIRIT, OR POLTERGEIST

From Ghost Detectors Malcolm and Dandy

16. Sometimes people are stuck where they died. Bring your specter detector everywhere you go.

17. Spook houses can be great places for poltergeists to hide. Be on watch for suspicious-looking mummies!

18. Animals are good indicators of supernatural activity. Watch them closely for unusual behavior.

19. Even without a specter detector, some ghosts can be seen. If you are lucky, the ghost you meet will be friendly!

20. No matter how careful you are, sometimes spirits just don't cooperate. Remember to watch out behind you. Being taken over by a spirit can give you a fright!